D1694615

Tacham Deowm & Linda Yotti

CROSS-OVER

BAUER-VERLAG

TACHAM DEOWM & LINDA YOTTI
CROSS-OVER

POETRY BOOK

CROSS-OVER
by Tacham Deowm & Linda Yotti
Published by Bauer-Verlag GmbH
Gennachstraße 1
D-87677 Thalhofen
www.verlag-bauer.de

Unless otherwise noted, all Scripture quotations are from the Holy Bible, New International Version. Copyright © 1973, 1978, Bible Society. Scripture quotations marked NLT are taken from the Holy Bible, New Living Translation, copyright ©1996, 2004, 2007 by Tyndale House Foundation. Used by permission of Tyndale House Publishers, Inc., Carol Stream, Illinois 60188. All rights reserved.

Graphic design by Renate Schlicht
Cover design by Renate Schlicht
www.renateschlicht.de
Photos by Thorsten Bonnensen, Tacham Deowm, Linda Yotti, Bret Yotti, Hilda Talsik, Thomas Tratnik and Marcel Extra

© 2014 by
Tacham Deowm & Linda Yotti
All rights reserved
ISBN: 978-3-95551-064-0

Foreword

It was a simple coffee date on a warm summer's day in August of 2013. We were chatting about nothing in particular. As we were sipping on our cold drinks, enjoying a few biscuits, the conversation turned to creative pursuits. In a moment of self-disclosure, we discovered that we both wrote poetry.

That moment was the spark that ignited and fanned into flame the book you now hold in your hand.

With this book, we are crossing over into new territory. We hope you will be inspired and cross over into new, undiscovered areas in your own life.
We hope you discover truths and dreams that were always there but you just never saw. We hope that this book opens new doors of faith and awakens the sleeping giant within you.

Deowm & Linda

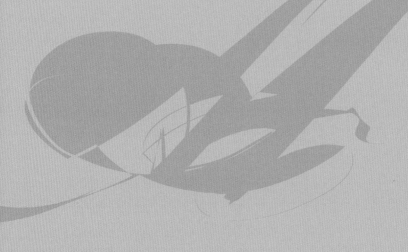

**Beautiful words stir my heart.
I will recite a lovely poem about the king,
for my tongue is like the pen of a skillful poet.**

Psalm 45:1 (Holy Bible, New Living Translation)

City of Faith, Hope and Love
Through the cracks ...

Above the grey city sky lies HOPE.
Surrounding every busy street, every agitated push
and scuffle and every baby's high-pitched squeal.
Here, in the midst of the grey monotony and brown
decay is ...
LOVE.
Blossoming between the pavement's cracks. Love is
in a bus driver's smile or a singing sparrow sitting on
a grey balcony.

Love is in the smell of a home-cooked meal when I
step inside the door to my flat. My husband's
dancing eyes draw me in.
And as I breathe this steely air, I feel a touch of
FAITH.

Through the seemingly unscalable walls surrounding
my life, an eagle comes to pick me up, lifts my eyes
to see far beyond the drudgery of daily life.

I see lands of HOPE and I am filled with LOVE as I
soar on wings of FAITH.

As my eyes grow accustomed to the light, I see that
my life is only a small part of a huge mosaic that
unfolds before my eyes.

Linda

DO NOT TRY

Do not try to look for God in the past
nor try to find him in the future
if you really want to find and experience God
you can discover Him in the now,
because you are limited to it
you are made for the present and herein you will find
His presence

BUT

that does not mean that God was not in the past
nor that He won't be in the future
He will
because He was, and He is, and He is to come
He is transcendent

RECKON

if time could limit Him, time would be God
but He is timeless
He has no beginning and no end
He has always been and He will always be
the Great I AM

DO NOT TRY

to find God in the failures of the past
in the hateful works and deeds of man
for you will not find Him there
He cannot be found in evil

BECAUSE

He is love
and therefore He can only be found in acts of love
sometimes you see people carrying a label
but it isn't real

if you see a Christian whose life is not marked by:
love, joy, peace, gentleness, kindness, goodness,
patience and faithfulness
believe me, he or she isn't real
they are just carrying His name!

do not try
to explain God
because you can't

THINK

if you could wholly explain God with your brain
and break Him down to your reason
God would be the object of your analysis!
but who are you, man of crises?
trying to figure out who God is
only to be at peace

CEASE

you do not even understand yourself
the things you do and don't do
better leave this matter to itself
or you are doomed to fall
like Satan, who tried to ascend to the highest heaven
to be like God
he wanted to be worshipped
and be someone he was never created to be
instead he was stripped
he fell and with him all
who are trying to be something or someone
they were never supposed to be

REALIZE

it takes humility
the recognition of our fragility
the comprehension of our weakness
that gives you the meekness

to boldly cry out for the redemption of your soul
to be made whole, from head to toe
and become a man
perfected and accepted by God
a being after His likeness

THEREFORE

Be yourself
Be human!

Deowm

Takeover of the mind

silent footsteps making their way
into hearts and minds
quietly, stealthily
thoughts nest in our minds
undetected
lying words burn into our consciousness
driving our actions
in every way
eradication is necessary
militant action
freeing the mind from its prison

Word slicing, hammering, breaking
and setting me free

Hidden Truths becoming alive,
as I let my heart feed on the Word, it grows,
touches, initiates action,
gives me courage

Rising in me is a counter-force,
pushing back the darkness,
bringing order and peace

Soon, there'll be a takeover of Light

Linda

Place me like a seal over your heart,
like a seal on your arm;
for love is as strong as death, its jealousy
unyielding as the grave.

It burns like blazing fire,
like a mighty flame.

Many waters cannot quench love;
rivers cannot sweep it away.

If one were to give
all the wealth of one's house for love,
it would be utterly scorned.

Song of Songs 8:6-7

MY BELOVED

While the soldiers played dice for your garment,
You paid the price for my predicament
and gave me your mantle of righteousness.

YOU

clothed me with a priceless gown
this lifts me up, even when I am down.
Through Your precious blood
that floods like a mighty river into all the world,
You delivered sinners,
this is spiritual truth for beginners.

This is my beloved,
He is the Lord of Life.
Besides Him there is no other God,
nor brother, sister or friend.
He is even greater than my mother!

He sticks closer to me than anyone could ever,
because it is He who lives and moves in me.
His breath of life is now in my body
sorry buddy

BUT
I got clever
and realized that it is He
who makes me complete,
not you.

I'll take back that shoe;
it was never your role
not even mine
to sit on His throne.

AT LAST
I have understood that He wants my heart,
more than the bravest knight or Robin Hood,
who competes for my heart at night.

RIGHT
this gives me the bravery
to move out of slavery,
the fear of man and of the enemy.
It gives me the freedom
to enter into His kingdom
and completely entrust my heart to His dominion.

TRUST
because he formed my heart
and understands all of its vulnerability and capability,
to store up every motion and emotion
from a fallen world and people.
He knows how to keep it safe and tender
and free from the devil's agenda.

THAT'S WHY
my heart belongs to my beloved
and His heart belongs to me.
United there is no force in heaven and on earth
that can stand against what our intimacy can birth.
LOVE-LIFE

Deowm

The Sounds of Life

Quiet. Just the sound of birds.
Gracing the pale blue sky with their chatter,
their song of life.

A piece of perfection, a slice of beauty.
Freely given as a blessing and a gift.

Massive birch tree swaying to a gentle breeze,
dancing to the rhythm of the earth.

All are dancers, following a carefully
choreographed piece.

Gracious Generous Giving God

graciously, generously giving us the gift of life,
every single day.

All are dancers, following a carefully
choreographed piece.

Gracious Generous Giving God

graciously, generously giving us the gift of life,
every single day.

Linda

Before you ever ...

Before you ever did anything good
I declared that you were very good
Before you ever called out my name
I called you by name and said that you were mine

Before you ever could say the words
"I love you Abba"
I loved you with an everlasting love
Before you ever asked Me for forgiveness
of your sins
I already forgave all of your sins on the cross,
remember?
Before you ever decided to give Me your life
I decided to give you my life
Before you ever gave Me any praise
I ordained that from the lips of babes, I will receive
my praise!

Just as a father loves his child who cannot yet say
"I love you" right
In the same way I love you and receive your love

I love you for I made you
I know you by heart
And now I want you to know me by heart!

Deowm

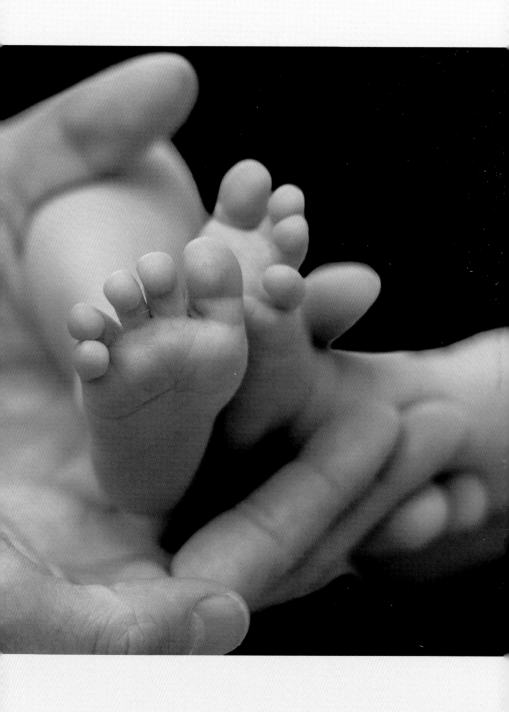

He prevailed

Although his name was scandalized
His works scrutinized and criticized
His figure personalized
Bound He was led to the tree
crucified and disfigured he set the captives free

He prevailed
and can adopt the most corrupt
invest in those we arrest
reframe and rename them as He did with Saul
who was a persecutor and hater
but later became the apostle Paul
the saint in chains who wrote letters out of prison
for the cause of freedom for all men!

I see a day of revival coming
prisoners free
a day were we will again receive letters out of prison
where the bound set the captives free
I see a day coming
where all God's children are free!

Deowm

broken again

there is a brokenness that leads to fruitfulness
a brokenness that leads to healing
a brokenness that creates tenderness

Christ's body was broken for us
so that we who have been excluded
could be included and found in Him

His life is like a piece of bread to be shared
a grape that was pressed into wine
and left to the side
so we can share Holy Come-union

there is a brokenness without selfishness
a brokenness that leads to
repentance and selfnessness
there is no openness without brokenness

Deowm

Unless a kernel of wheat falls to the ground and dies, it remains only a single seed. But if it dies, it produces many seeds.

John 12:24

Seasons of the Soul

seasons of DARKNESS
of seemingly disconnected parts
fuzziness and floating
not landing
standing on precipices
looking into yawning abysses
chills going down my spine
so heavy

seasons of LIGHT
airy soul
breathes easily
like sponge cake
dances and songs
orchestras and choirs
fullness and wonder
picking out stars
so beautiful

Linda

Humus

It's autumn.
The leaves have turned yellow, orange and brown.
And have fallen to the ground.
Dead.
It's dark and cold.
A pile of dead leaves cover the stump of the tree.
Leaves carried away by every gust of wind.
Stripped of their bloom.
They were green once.
Majestic and adored.
Stretching out to the sun.
Now it is dark.
Both man and beast trample upon leaves with haste and no regard for their former state.
Soon they will lose their form and turn into humus.

The leaves remind me of the homeless.
They too are fading away like dead leaves.
Lying at the corners of our streets.
We pass them by in a hurry and with no regard for their former state.
Could there possibly be something beautiful about the homeless?
Life has given them a deadly blow.
Dropped by their own kind, they are piled together like dead leaves.
Because they have become useless.
Reduced to the lowest form of existence.
Soon, they too will return to humus.

Death & Life

Born to die but
destined to live

Born in sin
please forgive

Born in nakedness
now clothed with splendor like Dior

Life is good and bad
that makes me sad
but
I have got a choice to make
and there is something good to take

Don't be shy
look up to the sky

Do you remember the movie "Seven"?
That is not heaven!
Never
His love reaches to the heavens
That's why I want to go to heaven
Need his love more than ever
Now listen to me,
Life
is a like a breeze
Breathe
in
and
out
and
you
are
out
and
into
eternity!

Deowm

The Dancer

the beautiful dancer
is jumping, dancing, twirling
expressing what is inside

the dancer is agile and quick
nimble and light-footed

like lightning through the sky
lighting up the night

the dancer is like a cat
moving stealthily through the night
carefully with soft, quiet steps

the dancer is in every quickened heart
every soul that's been kissed awake by Him

Linda

Collision

Hope and Despair are standing
across from each other
>Despair is pushing, but Hope wants in

Fear and Love are staring each other down
>Who will win?

Points of collision
>Uncomfortable contact

Heaviness wants to stay but Joy barges in
>Gracious encroachment of light

Will you let the Voice be louder?

Exchange the shame, exchange the lies, break through your shell of pain

Be born again .....

into New Hope, Joy and Peace, surrounded by Love

Purpose in your Heart,
Fearless steps and Beauty in your smile

THIS is your new reality

Linda

I AM

I am, yet I'm struggling to be ME
and not you for you

But who am I?
I know what he and she and you
and what they say
but that is not who I am

I am more than my looks
and the books I read

I'm worth more than the money I earn
and what I have learned
I am more than my achievements or failures

For I have been made by the "Great I Am"
to be who I am
for Him and perhaps for you
to be ME
because
he's already got you   Deowm

Precious

Something of value
worth
honoured and loved
caressed and intimately known
hand-carved, crafted and put together by the One

Worth comes from Him alone
Destined to fly, to shine,
to serve and to love

Like a precious stone
A diamond in the rough
being polished every day

Worth

You have it

Just because you're you

And because you're His alone

Linda

My God

You drew me out of deep waters
and pulled me out of my mother's loins.
Over and over and over
You rescued me out of fire and dangerous places.
From the deepest pit
and the highest height
You brought me to my knees
and gave me the will to live again.

Deowm

Through darkened eyes ...

The view through these glasses is so dark –
I can't see you, can't even see myself
Where are you? Why can't I see you?
I feel blind, deaf and dumb
Inhibited and closed in
Frightened like a deer
Afraid like a zebra being hunted down
Squashed, pushed, pulled
Someone is living my life
It's just not me
Where am I?
Can't feel my own heart anymore
Gone numb and cold
Functioning
Talking without really communicating
Hearing words but not really listening
Walking, talking, sleeping, eating
Is this all there is to life?
One day I awaken to find the shades have lifted
I can see a bit clearer now
I can see Your face again
Can feel the breeze on my cheeks
see the sunset float down through the clouds
Sense Your touch
feel Your words again
touch your face
and know ...
I am ALIVE

Linda

The Choice

Perception, depth, quality of life
So much hinges on choice

Step this way or that

Choose the red or the yellow pill

Go up or down
Left or right

You can colour your world
with your thoughts

Paste it together with memories

... or you can leave it as it is ...

unexamined, routine-like and grey

Dare to pick up the paintbrush and be a painter.

Linda

For if, by the trespass of the one man, death reigned through that one man, how much more will those who receive God's abundant provision of grace and of the gift of righteousness reign in life through the one man, Jesus Christ!

Romans 5:17

I see Men

I see men all around
confused · insecure · angry
shrewd · shy · lost
stripped of their dignity
who fear nothing but are afraid of everything.

I see men hiding behind work
clothes · position · and women
bored · tired · not inspired
to be courageous and daring men
fat · thick · small · tall · big · short
all alike not wanted!

Because they are playing it safe
instead of being brave
few have got power but won't share it
instead they dominate to escalate.

I see broken men
hustlers · gang-bangers · whoremongers · preachers
teachers · bus drivers · tycoons
co-workers · dealers · doctors · pimps
strippers · economists · politicians
and bankers …
Searching for affirmation
but where are their fathers?
Hooked up · shut down · locked up · in jail
dead · silent · busy · not here!

Who cares?

There are boys who need to be taught by fathers
girls looking for their fathers in other men
women who are fighting and have taken up
masculinity in this promiscuity
where there is no responsibility.

Yet I see men
who are searching for truth
fathering even though they had no fathers
men who fear God
men who are not afraid of other men

I see men of standard
integrity · ability · stability
men of honor
who know how to use their power
men of hope faith and love
men of war and peace

Men of great sacrifices
for their families and society
Men of dignity

Deowm

Women

We have been called to shape the world
with our words
instead we are hung up on words like
he loves me, he loves me not
and live to shape our figures
that's bitter

We are meant to be a mystery
and not an open book for all to read
a beautiful poem and not a dictionary, porn leaflet or
bad news

Time to get serious
we have been created for God's holiness
and not to fill men's loneliness

We're called to be life-givers, nurturers, lovers,
mothers, psalmists and supporters
and not life-takers, beggars, haters,
women with children, gossipers and backbiters

Diamond ring, gold chain, lip stick, hand bag,
perfume, fine cloth and the like,
can't make up for
love, respect and honor
we get our nails done, hair straight
but when are we going to get our heart in order?

Time to wake up from our hangover
and get a real makeover
Spirit, Soul and Body

There is a peeling
that leads to healing
a touch, a hug and kiss
that means more than the title Miss

It's the embrace of our Father
our Lover and King
He knows our origin and femininity
from eternity He has called us to be His
precious daughters and bride
without a reason to hide

Time to discover our captivating beauty
which has nothing to do with nudity
or being haughty or naughty

We have been blessed
to be nothing less than princesses and queens
even in our late teens
He considers us priceless, blameless and flawless

Women
We are most dear, most welcomed, most loved
most desired, most cherished and wanted
This is who you we are to Him.

Deowm

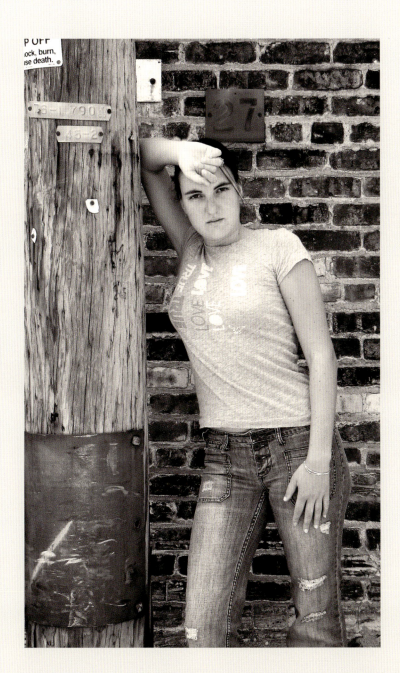

Africa arise

Africa arise and rediscover your face
You have been beaten down and knocked out
Severely wounded but STILL alive!
Africa arise and tell me your story

Who were you before you were exploited?
What was your expression like
before you were distorted?
Before the many lashes and tears?

Africa arise and tell me your story
Can you recover your own beauty?
And lay aside the ugly face of your defeat
That others want you to keep

Africa, you were meant to be distinctively different
For you are uniquely gifted, vibrant and intelligent
Africa arise, awake from your stupor
And clothe yourself with vigor
You have embraced the world
Now it is time for you to embrace yourself
Africa arise, discover your Lover
Though you have been slain, yet put your trust in Him

ARISE to your God-given strength to be a mother
You were never meant to be beggar
You are a giver and it is time for you to deliver
Agents of change and children of hope!
Africa arise to write another story
HIStory

YOU

Talking to you is like drinking a cold beer
on a hot summer's day
Sharing my heart is like emptying my closet
or giving away a precious gown
Listening to you is as pleasing as buying a new dress
on SALE.

My soul floats like a boat on quiet waters
Your laughter rocks my boat
Like a fisherman catches fish
I'm enabled to catch grandiose thoughts
which usually slip away, like slippery fish.

I can make perfect sense of nonsense
and forget about what did not make sense
during my day.

Timeless chatter which makes things better,
meaningful, yet light as biscuit
Therefore, I do not want to quit talking to YOU.

Deowm

FAITH

He's worth trusting

When you believe, you start running
blindly trusting
Tripping over stones and through dark valleys
Moving up steep cliffs
Just a wall going straight down under you

Do you believe Him?
Or do you doubt?

He's worth trusting

When you see a small hill after the valley,
surrounded by light, vibrantly green and alive
Or when you see the beautiful scenery from above,
as far as the eye can see

Then your heart overflows with joy and thanksgiving
And the roots of faith grow a little deeper

He's worth trusting.

Linda

Excavation

who can discover the depth of a human soul?
its longing, yearning, crying for exploration
what man or woman is not afraid of exploitation?

for to discover is to uncover

novelties, long hidden trash and ashes
from the past, traces of genius fabrication
buried in fear and doubt

the daring who are caring are sharing
from their deepest soul,
things that almost can't be entrusted
to another soul
because they are too lofty, heavy and scary

who can stand the scrutiny and judgment
of the explorer?
his wondering eyes and fright, amazement and
gladness that can easily turn into madness
if it is not harnessed like a horse

people whose souls are never discovered
become harder and darker
because no light of interest has fallen onto them
some live and die and have never been discovered
yet you have been called to live in the light

Deowm

Beauty

is more than just being attractive,
it is the ability to be pleasing to another.

Deowm

Generous

Generous openness.
Soft ways and beautiful gestures. Mysterious look.
Loving eyes. Dancing melodies surround you.
Woman of beauty and grace.
For you know who you are. You know who you are. You know that life is meant to be enjoyed and savoured.

Man of victory. Steadfastness in your steps.
Eyes of secure conviction. Steps of surety.
The Voice leads and guides.
Helps you be. Helps you be.
Man of courage.

Linda

In times like these

In times like these
when my love for you is cold
heart hardened, vision faded
my will for righteousness gone
darkness overshadows me
and I feel all alone

In times like these
You are still with me
Your rod and Your staff lead me
right back to Your heart of love

A table you set before me
right in the midst of my enemies
You call me to dine and hand me new wine
You name me favorite and ask me to be Thine
now my heart begins to throb and leap for joy
overflowing with thankfulness
because of your forgiveness and tenderness

In times like these
I want to kiss your feet, touch Your hands
never cease to look into Your lovely face
it is when I realize that there was no reason to hide
for next to Your loving arms
in the heat of Your love and grace
I have my place
here you satisfy my every need

Deowm

Life in moments

Baking muffins. Flying to the US. Taking a bike ride. Making calls to offices. Kissing. Trying to find myself. Nurturing friendships. Going to bed. Listening for sounds. Painting nails. Discovering new worlds. Watering plants. Wiping the kitchen counter. Skyping or whatsapping. Going through the shopping list in my head. Trying to be happy. Getting out of the bus. Standing on the train. Watching the skyline. Using my EC-card. Listening to songs in my head. Trying out a new shampoo. Worrying. Getting wet. Eating pizza. Writing down words. Dancing through the living room. Laying everything before Him. In the knowledge that He's the author of this mosaic. This adventure. What is behind the next door?

Linda

Truly I tell you, if you have **faith** as SMALL as a **mustard seed**, you can say to this mountain, "Move from here to there", and it will move. Nothing will be impossible for you.

Matthew 17:20

Concluding words

Words words words ...

Words are powerful, words shape our lives. Many people are hung up on words, mostly negative and destructive ones. Rarely do you encounter people who are hung up on positive words. Like a piece of cloth on a washing line, they have been immobilised, fixated, caught up in the air by words.

In order to move forward, we need to be free and grounded. Therefore, it is time to take up the scissors and cut through the washing line. As the words drop to the ground, pick up the letters and create your own world. For death and life are in the power of your tongue.

We hope that this book has inspired you to be hung up on what is beautiful, noble and positive.

Words are powerful. You can change your life if you change your words!

Deowm & Linda

About Linda Yotti

Linda Yotti was born in Cape Town, South Africa. Growing up in multicultural South Africa in a German-speaking family helped her develop a love and an interest for different languages and cultures at an early age. She took her first trip to Germany with her family in 1991. She majored in German and English at the university of Stellenbosch, going on to do two Master's degrees.

She has written poetry in her spare time for as long as she can remember and is fascinated by the power of words. She especially draws her inspiration from songs. Linda is married to Bret, they currently make their home in Frankfurt am Main.

About Tacham Deowm

Tacham Deowm spent her early childhood years on the African continent, in a little village in Cameroon called Bamumbu. One of a family of 15, she immigrated to Germany in the year of the fall of the Berlin Wall. This was her very personal turning point.

She is a remedial teacher and holds a Bachelor's degree in education. Today she lives in Frankfurt am Main and leads a day care facility for primary school pupils. Deowm is a passionate photographer with an unique eye for people and an author of several picture book stories. Her heart is to see people develop in every way.

Picture Credits

Cover Photo	Linda Yotti
Picture 1, Psalm 45:1	Linda Yotti
Picture 2, City of Faith, Hope and Love	Linda Yotti
Picture 3, Do not try	Tacham Deowm
Picture 4, Do not try	Tacham Deowm
Picture 5, Do not try	Linda Yotti
Picture 6, Takeover of the mind	Tacham Deowm
Picture 7, Takeover of the mind	Tacham Deowm
Picture 8, Song of Songs 8:6-7	Unknown
Picture 9, My Beloved	Hilda Talsik
Picture 10, Sounds of Life	Tacham Deowm
Picture 11, Before you ever	Thorsten Bonnesen
Picture 12, Broken again	Linda Yotti
Picture 13, Seasons of the Soul	Tacham Deowm
Picture 14, Humus	Thorsten Bonnesen
Picture 15, Death & Life	Tacham Deowm
Picture 16, The Dancer	Thorsten Bonnesen
Picture 17, Collision	Tacham Deowm
Picture 18, I am	Tacham Deowm
Picture 19, Through darkened eyes	Thorsten Bonnesen
Picture 20, I see Men	Tacham Deowm
Picture 21, Women	Tacham Deowm
Picture 22, Africa arise	Tacham Deowm
Picture 23, Excavation	Tacham Deowm
Picture 24, Beauty	Bret Yotti
Picture 25, Matthew 17:20	Thorsten Bonnesen
Picture 26, Concluding words	Bret Yotti
Picture 27, About Linda Yotti	Thomas Tratnik
Picture 28, About Tacham Deowm	Marcel Extra

Contents

Foreword	7
Psalm 45:1	8
City of Faith, Hope and Love	10
Do not try	12
Takeover of the mind	19
Song of Songs 8: 6-7	22
My Beloved	24
The Sounds of Life	28
Before you ever ...	30
He prevailed	33
Broken again	34
John 12:24	35
Seasons of the Soul	37
Humus	39
Death & Life	40
The Dancer	42
Collision	44
I am	46
Precious	48
My God	49
Through darkened eyes ...	50
The Choice	52
Romans 5:17	53
I see Men	55
Women	57
Africa arise	61
You	62
Faith	63
Excavation	65
Beauty	67
Generous	67
In times like these	68
Life in moments	69
Matthew 17:20	70
Concluding words	73
About Linda Yotti	74
About Tacham Deowm	75